A Ship-load of Sea Stories
&
1 Fairy Tale

By

Larry Laswell

Copyright © MMXV Marshell Publishing
All rights reserved.

ISBN-13: 978-0-9863853-3-9

Now Hear This . . .

I was lucky, the navy's recruiting slogan, "It's not just a job, it's an adventure," held true for me. Yes, there were hardships, and I had to deal with people shooting at me (once by an unreasonably upset and jealous husband, but that's a different story). Nevertheless, my navy experience was truly an adventure, and I would be the first to admit I am better for it. After forty years, it's time to share a few of my adventures.

One of the first things I learned in the navy was the difference between a sea story and a fairy tale. Tradition dictates that fairy tales begin with the phrase "Once upon a time," and sea stories begin with the phrase "Now this ain't no shit." You see, a sea story is bona fide fact devoid of exaggeration or embellishment, whereas a fairy tale is—well, a fairy tale.

The traditions of trustworthiness regarding sea stories are so sacred that no one can recall any instance in which someone questioned the rectitude of a sea story. No shit. I felt compelled to distinguish between the two types of stories lest the reader get the wrong idea about the veracity of the following collection of stories.

What follows are snippets from my adventure in the US Navy as I remember them, or as I imagine I remember them. I leave it to the reader to separate fact from fairy tale, but in the spirit of full disclosure, the reader should know that the older I get, the better I was.

Below the copyright statement my attorney demanded I add wording to the effect that this is a work of fiction (fairy tale) and any resemblance to a sea story (historical fact) is purely coincidental. Even though my attorney claims the statute of limitations protects me, he still insists I call this a collection of fairy tales, which is a good idea because the navy has a long memory and a poor sense of humor. It is also fitting that I apologize in advance to those who think they recognize themselves.

Now that I have that off my chest, let's begin.

Now this ain't no shit. It was 1967 and . . .

And on the seventh day, God rested.

*On the eighth day, God realized the heavens and
earth were without mirth,*

so he created the US Navy.

Economic Odds

During the Vietnam War, flunking college courses could be troublesome if you were a male. There was this thing, an especially cherished thing, called a student 4-S draft deferment. Lose that and your draft status went to 1-A, which meant you were headed to Vietnam; your departure date just hadn't been established yet.

The cherished 4-S student deferment was granted to all college students in good academic standing. The most important part of the previous sentence is, *in good academic standing.* Unfortunately, in my first year at Toledo University I majored in party. I was an excellent student in the Art of Party, but I flunked those droll things the university called classes. Soon my *good standing* was lost and, presto, I became 1-A.

I was drafted on a Thursday in April of my second semester. I remember it was a Thursday because that was the day all ROTC students had to wear their army uniforms. When I arrived home from my last class of the day, I stopped at the end of the driveway to pick up the mail. Awaiting me were the dreaded greetings from the president and an invitation to report for a complete physical, courtesy of the government.

Thirty minutes later I marched into the navy recruiting office in the downtown Federal Building, found the first person who looked official, and announced, "I'm here to enlist in the navy."

A petty officer first class, in his impeccable blue navy jumper, looked up and smiled. The smile slowly dissolved as he scanned me and my Army ROTC dress uniform from head to toe. He then uttered the only intelligent thought that came to his mind, "Huh?"

"I'm here to enlist in the navy. Where do I sign up."

"You're in the army, aren't you?" Mr. Petty Officer Sir said.

"Oh, this uniform isn't real. It's just an ROTC uniform. I decided I like the navy, so I'm quitting college to go to sea."

"Lost your 4-S deferment, did you?"

"Well, yes, but that's not why I'm here. I'm tired of this college and army stuff. I want to go to sea. Just show me where to sign."

Two hours later after an interview, several tests, and a mountain of paperwork, I finally signed my name to a piece of paper that officially made me a genuine swabbie. Relieved, I collected my official paperwork and marched across the hall to my draft board office. A nice old lady greeted me with a warm, broad smile that is the specialty of grandmothers worldwide: "May I help you, sir?"

I handed her my draft notice. "Yes, there has been a mistake. I got drafted, but I'm in the navy."

"You mean you're in the army," she corrected.

"No, I'm in the navy," and I handed her my official navy documents.

She looked at the draft notice, the navy paperwork, then at my uniform. "Oh dear, I think I need to talk to my supervisor," she said, and she trundled off to the rear of the office.

It turned out the supervisor was a jillion years old with paper thin white skin and slicked back, jet black hair. He could've played Dracula without makeup. He explained he had a quota to fill, and he intended to nullify my navy enlistment. To do that he needed to fill out some government forms that required an extensive interview with the draftee.

In an obscure eight-by-eight room with two chairs, a small table, and a single ceiling light bulb, an intense interrogation ensued; Count Dracula wasn't about to let my head not count toward his quota. Dracula knew he had bagged me first, and he wasn't going to let the navy have my head without a fight. Sensing my plight, grandma bustled her way across the hall to retrieve Mister Petty Officer Sir. Soon it became clear he had a quota as well, and he was not about to let the Count have my head for his count.

An argument ensued, and just when I thought things were going to get bloody, grandma intervened to mediate a compromise. The navy could have my body, but my head belonged to Dracula so the Count could count my head. Thank you, grandmothers everywhere.

Some may assume my enlistment that afternoon was a brash, impetuous act. Not so; it had been well thought out. I figured the army gave you a $120 rifle, and if it lost you, the most the government would be out would be a hundred and twenty bucks. But the navy puts you on a $16 million ship, and if they lost the ship and you, they would be out some serious folding money. You see, I had concluded my economic odds of surviving the Vietnam War were better in the navy. After all, my father had taught me, "When you don't know what to do, follow the money."

Off to Sea the World

When I joined the navy, little did I realize I had forfeited the right to America's founding principles: life, liberty, and the pursuit of decent airline reservations. I was about to realize that to save a buck fifty-eight, the navy would ignore common sense, go right past stupid, and score a direct hit on f*&@!)%= dumb.

When the day came for me to report to boot camp, Mister Petty Officer Sir drove me from Toledo to the Cleveland airport. (For those of you who are wondering, yes, Toledo has an airport.) The recruiter gave me a voucher to present at the airline desk to pay for my ticket to San Diego. (For those of you who are wondering, yes, Great Lakes would have been much closer.)

At eight in the morning, he dropped me at the curb. I was truly on my own in a strange land. I could feel the aura of adultness glowing around me when I presented the voucher to the airline clerk, who examined the voucher, frowned, and said, "Are you sure this is right?"

"What do you mean?"

"This voucher routes you from Cleveland, to Memphis, to St. Louis, to Denver, to Phoenix, to Los Angeles, then to San Diego. We have a nonstop to San Diego leaving two minutes later."

"No kidding. Give me the nonstop."

The clerk started fumbling with catalog-sized books and said, "I can't figure out why they did that." After much page flipping, scratching out notes, and doing some arithmetic, he looked at me astonished. "This routing is a dollar fifty-eight cheaper than the direct flight."

That was no problem. I reached in my pocket and presented the clerk with a $5 bill.

The clerk looked apologetic: "Can't do that; there is no way to do the accounting. Government regulations, you see." (For those of you who are wondering, yes, the navy probably paid some GS-3 overtime to figure out how to save a buck fifty-eight.)

So it came to pass that twenty-three hours later I arrived in San Diego, a day older, wiser, and sleepier. During one of the layovers it occurred to me that the words "navy" and "common sense" are mutually exclusive.

Boot Camp

*And on the ninth day, God realized there was no hell
on earth, so he created boot camp.*

Remember how friendly Mister Petty Officer Sir was to me? He told me lots of funny sea stories, and he took the time out of his busy day to drive me to Cleveland to catch my flight to San Diego. In retrospect, I would learn Mister Petty Officer Sir was not my friend, and neither was the second petty officer I met, and he was a chief petty officer.

For me, boot camp was an unceremonious in-your-face, kick-in-the-ass introduction to the real world. Ripped from the protective womb of family and home, I was thrust into a world where no one gives a shit about you, what you think, or how you feel, no matter how friendly he may seem. So there I was in San Diego after my twenty-three-hour flight, tired, groggy, sweaty, and stinky at oh-dark hundred in the morning. Despite my apprehension, I knew everything was going to be all right. I was on my own and, for the first time in my life, I felt like a man.

Yesterday had been a big day for me, saying good-bye to my mother, father, and brother. Now in the San Diego Airport I had scrupulously followed the recruiter's instructions and had brought no luggage other than a small athletic bag containing a few toilet articles and a towel. Mister Petty Officer Sir had told me it didn't matter what I wore, so anticipating that I would meet many new friends my own age, I had dressed comfortably in shorts, a Hawaiian shirt, and sandals. After all, I was going to sunny California.

When I reached the main baggage claim area, I looked for the navy ground transportation liaison sign as instructed. I saw the small kiosk set in the center of a large open area with the sign above it. Inside the kiosk sat a beautiful, smiling WAVE tending a phone and several clipboards.

Outside the kiosk, an important looking man paced patiently. He was old, but maybe a little younger than my grandfather. He looked impressive in his blue uniform, which was covered with a bewildering array of insignia, ribbons, and gold stripes. Maybe I could look like that some day.

I walked directly up to him and boldly stuck my hand out to introduce myself. "Excuse me. I'm Larry Laswell. The recruiter told me to check in with you."

The elder man turned and greeted me with a big, warm grin. "Laswell? Welcome to the navy. Would you follow me, please?"

The WAVE nodded to the older man and made a mark on one of her clipboards. As we walked through the terminal, the older man asked how my flight had been and engaged in friendly small talk until we stepped outside, leaving the milling crowd of civilians behind in the terminal. The older man had led me through a side door, which seemed natural; navy men would get special treatment and have shortcuts denied to civilians.

Outside we were in a small, sidewalk-rimmed parking lot. When we reached the curb, the older man turned on me and in a stern, angry voice yelled, "Okay, squirrel. You see the man down there by the bus? Report to him—on the double, dweeb. That means now!"

Stunned by the sudden change in my new friend, I stared at him dumbstruck. The elder man had little patience. "I said now, slimeball!"

Wounded, I began to walk toward the gray navy bus. From behind me the older man screamed, "I said *now*! That means on the double! Run!"

I broke into a sprint, and the other man raced to meet me. As we ran toward the bus together, the other man screamed in my face, "Okay, squirrel. You're in the navy now. No more mama. Fall in with the others at attention. You'll see footprints painted on the concrete. Put your left foot in the left footprint and your right foot in the right footprint. Put your bag down next to your right foot and come to attention. When you're at attention, you will not twitch, you will not move, you will not blink, you will not scratch, you will not talk, you will not pass gas, you will not do anything—not even think—unless I tell you to. Do you understand, squirrel?"

I did my best to comply with the barrage of instructions and replied, "Yeah."

"What? What did you say, loon lips?" he screamed. "You mean, 'Yes, sir,' don't you?"

"Yes, sir?" I mumbled

"I can't hear you, whale turd. What'd you say?"

"Yes, sir!" I yelled as loudly as I could.

Silence returned. I didn't think boot camp would be like this. Maybe I'd made a mistake. The man looked away for a second, then spun to glare at me. "Did you say something, bubble brain?"

"No, sir!"

Standing at attention, I tried to make my mind go blank, but a thought kept spinning: *Friends who outrank you aren't.*

The Grinder

Among our nation's founding principles is pursuit of happiness. That presupposes there is an element of fairness and justice in society. But in boot camp, fairness is a four-letter word.

The sun was just coming up when the navy bus from the airport careened through the navy base gate. I was still licking my wounds from my friends' betrayal, but my mood began to improve. Things weren't going to be too bad after all.

As we drove across the base, the view from the bus was stunning. The San Diego Recruit Depot and Training Center was one of the most beautiful places I had ever beheld. The wide, graceful, tree-lined streets immediately put you at ease. The Spanish architecture—white adobe buildings, red tile roofs, wide covered sidewalks behind graceful arches—added to the sense of charm and stately calm. With the light sea breezes and an ample supply of shade trees, spending time here would be like an afternoon in the park.

Then the bus turned a corner and headed for the bridge over the moat. (The "moat," as we called it, was a natural inlet off the San Diego harbor, but it served the navy's purpose, both physically and psychologically.) In front of us was a hellhole reserved exclusively for recruits like me. It looked like a Russian gulag; all asphalt and wired fences and two-story concrete block buildings. They might have made the buildings three stories, but being adjacent to the end of the airport runway, this would not have been a good idea. Just as the bus stopped, a jet roared overhead, and the landing gear cleared the top of the barracks by no more than ten feet. No shit: ten feet.

"What if something bad happens when a plane lands?" I asked the bus driver.

"Who cares? What's a few recruits more or less?"

The Induction and Recruit Training center were relegated to the distant backwaters of the base to keep us squirrels away from polite civilization. It was at the induction center that I learned my name really was Squirrel. It had to be because that is what the drill instructor always called me. And by an amazing coincidence, every recruit in my group was named Squirrel—except one guy named Whale Turd. If my recruit company had been a wolf pack, Whale Turd would have been the omega wolf.

On my first day in the induction center I realized majoring in party had been a bad move. Around three in the afternoon, a handful of drill

9

instructors herded us out to The Grinder, a five-acre patch of asphalt upon which I would soon be spending many hours marching to and fro. It was called The Grinder because it was where the navy ground squirrels into fine talc-like powder from which it would mold them into sailors and give them back their family names.

We were ordered to police The Grinder and pick up anything that didn't look like asphalt. The futility of this was not lost on me. Unless there were units marching on The Grinder, there were at least a hundred men named Squirrel policing it. It was spotless to a fault.

Having only been in the navy a few hours, I still believed in logic. The drill instructors wanted to be sure The Grinder was clean. Give them that assurance, and all would be well. Eager to show my leadership potential (I had been in ROTC, after all), I stepped forward and took charge—not out of ego but out of sympathy for myself and my fellow Squirrels. I had a plan.

"Hey, everyone, let's go to the far end of the grinder and spread out across it. We can then walk the length of the grinder and pick up anything we find. One sweep and we'll be done!" I yelled.

Surprisingly, everyone complied. After we made our first sweep I ran back to the drill instructor, half expecting to be complimented for my leadership and efficiency, and proudly reported, "The grinder is clean, sir."

The fallacy of my plan and the inaccuracy of my statement became evident when another drill instructor took a puff of his cigarette and flicked the butt onto the grinder.

"I don't think so!" the drill instructor yelled. "You just gave me a false report, Squirrel. That'll cost you fifty."

"Fifty? Fifty dollars? I don't have fifty dollars," I pleaded.

"Push-ups, birdbrain. Drop and give me fifty."

After my fifty push-ups, we spent the next three hours walking back and forth across The Grinder, but all we found was a lone cigarette butt. You see, the navy is awash in fairness; you get as much shit as you can take.

Whale Turd

Whale Turd, my recruit company's omega recruit, had a medical deformity. Either by genetics or because of an accident, Whale Turd couldn't straighten his neck, so his head was always cocked to the right about twenty degrees. When at attention, your body has to be erect, head straight, and the bottom of your white hat has to be parallel with the deck. This made Whale Turd such an inviting target for sadistic drill instructors that we had a constant stream of DIs who visited solely for the enjoyment of picking on Whale Turd. It would go something like this:

"Come to attention, Whale Turd."

Whale Turd complied.

"Square you hat to the deck, Whale Turd."

Whale Turd cocked his hat to the left of his head so it was parallel to the deck.

"Get your head straight."

Whale Turd bent to the left, sideways, so his head was vertical.

"I said square your hat."

Whale Turd squared his hat.

"Stand up straight, Whale Turd."

Whale Turd straightened his body; his head cocked to the right.

"You must not be able to hear me, Whale Turd. Didn't I tell you to square your hat to the deck?"

Whale Turd cocked his hat to the left again so it was parallel to the deck. And so it would go, round and round for the next several minutes, until the drill instructor had satisfied his sadistic desires.

Like I said before, fairness was a four-letter word. Whale Turd got all the shit he could take.

Welcome to Medical

Boot camp was a meat grinder that spewed forth a string of neatly cased recruits for the fleet. Part of that process was making sure a recruit could be sent to any point on the globe without concern for preventable medical problems. The focus was on vaccinations and dental health. Those were high volume businesses, and assembly line techniques were put to full use. Before I go any further, let me state that the navy gave me the best medical care of my life—except for the time the assembly line malfunctioned.

Every so often we'd march to medical for another battery of shots. The process was simple, relatively painless, and quick. I'd queue up, take off my jumper and T-shirt, and wait. The room would be silent except for the pumpf, pumpf, pumpf of the air-powered injection guns the corpsmen used. When my turn came, I took two steps forward, and a corpsman on each side grabbed an arm and pulled the trigger—pumpf-pumpf. I'd take two steps forward, put my T-shirt and jumper back on, and wait. When my turn came again, I'd take two steps forward, drop trou, bend over, and pumpf-pumpf. I was done until the next week.

My first trip to dental wasn't as easy or efficient. The corpsman at the front door started by giving me an empty dental record folder. His goal was to get me out the back door as soon as possible with a complete dental record, including X-rays. The dental facility was a long, narrow building with a wide hallway down the middle. To each side of the hallway were about twenty numbered rooms.

I queued up outside of room number one and waited for a panoramic X-ray. Room two was next, and so on. Room four is where the X-rays were read and my problems began. I climbed into the dental chair and waited while the gum-chewing dentist with sunglasses found my X-ray and snapped it into the illuminated reading panel.

"We got a problem here," he pronounced, squinting at the panel. "You've got an impacted wisdom tooth. Gotta come out. Open up for a sec."

He checked the tooth. "Worse than I thought. Hasn't come through the gum yet. Gonna have to cut it, and then yank it."

He returned to the X-ray for a second and actually looked at me sympathetically. "This ain't your lucky day; the root's hooked around the jawbone. Go to room ten."

I already knew about the root problem because men in my family have molars with fishhook-shaped roots that curl around the jawbone. I trudged to room ten and got Novocain shots. In military terms, this was not a surgical strike; the dentist carpet bombed my lower left jaw with bunker-busters.

By the time I sat down in room thirteen, my lower left jaw was numb to the armpit. Without so much as a perfunctory hello, the dentist grabbed my lower jaw, clamped my tongue, yanked down, and hit my lower right jaw with something sharp.

"Ahaa ouc aaa!" I screamed.

Apparently you get all types of recruits in boot camp, and the dentists know exactly how to handle them. Without letting go of my jaw, he said, "Hold still; I'm not hurting you." Then toward the door he yelled, "Need some help in here."

Within seconds, two assistants, one on each side, were holding me down in the chair. The dentist hit me with the sharp object again, only worse.

"AHHHH GARUFFFF OU WRON SNYD!" I yelled as best I could with a mouth full of hands and a numb tongue. "Hold still," he ordered. Then he yelled toward the door: "Need some more help in here!"

Once I was satisfactorily immobilized by four assistants, the dentist climbed into my mouth with both hands, both feet, and a couple pounds of equipment; he cut my gum, crushed the tooth with something like vice grips, and picked the pieces of the tooth out one by one. Finally, he extracted his appendages and equipment, leaving behind a large lump of gauze.

"There, that wasn't so bad, was it?"

My head was spinning; there were spots in front of my eyes; I wasn't sure where I was, but I managed to say, "The shot was on the other side."

His jaw dropped. "Why didn't you tell me?"

"I tried."

"Can you get up?"

I could.

I did.

I passed out.

I woke up wearing an oxygen, mask and listened as the dentist apologized for the next ten minutes. To compensate me for pain and suffering he gave me two pieces of paper. The first excused me from all physical activity for twenty-four hours. Because it was boot camp, and it was only nine in the morning, that was valuable. But the second piece of paper was a treasure; it granted me unlimited ice cream privileges at the mess hall for three days. The navy only gave recruits ice cream once a week, even during the hot San Diego summer. That piece of paper made me the most popular man in my company. In the end, I was happy that the dentist removed the right tooth, and I didn't have to go back for an encore.

Seaman Recruit Cockroach

Anyone who has been aboard a ship at sea knows the navy runs on coffee. But that is only partly true because if the navy ran out of paper, I believe ships would be stranded at sea, and the bureaucracy would grind to a halt. In boot camp, paperwork became the bane of my existence until I realized if you fed the paper monster the right paperwork, good things would happen.

Boot camp had its trials and tribulations, but overall, I got off light. When my company was formed, I was appointed the company yeoman and given a new name, Yo Yo. This excused me from some manual labor, but to compensate I had to spend long hours filling out sick chits, rosters, and other paperwork in triplicate. There was always more paperwork, and it always had to be in triplicate.

Sick chits were for men who needed to go to the sick bay. They are similar to hall passes that gave individuals permission to travel to and from sick bay. Company rosters listing the status of all company personnel and their location had to be typed daily. Each morning at formation, it was my duty to present the roster to the inspecting officer.

On the morning of the Charlie Cockroach incident, my company had formed to await inspection. Three men going to sick bay stood to the side with their required ditty bags and sick chits. A ditty bag is a small muslin bag filled with toilet articles and a change of skivvies. As usual, I presented my roster and informed the inspecting officer the barracks were ready for inspection.

After inspection, the inspecting officer approached me. "Yo Yo, you have some problems. We found a dead cockroach in the shower. We see no cockroach listed on your company roster. The cockroach was out of uniform and needed a shave. Being dead, he was obviously sick, but we found neither a sick chit for him nor his ditty bag. Furthermore, said cockroach was not in formation but in the barracks at the time of inspection, which is against regulations. Finally, you reported the barracks was ready for inspection, and it wasn't. That's a total of nine infractions, which is unacceptable. What do you have to say for yourself?"

Things couldn't get much worse. Bravery was needed to stare down this enemy. "Sir, there are no cockroaches assigned to our company."

"Are you saying your company security is so lax anyone can just wander into your shower room?" the officer asked.

Things had just gotten worse.

15

"No, sir."

"Then what are you saying?"

I had forgotten about the mutually exclusive relationship between the navy and logic. It occurred to me we were being framed, which was illogical, but this was the navy, which made it perfectly logical. With total disregard for the lessons already learned, I lawyered up. Why I did this remains a mystery to this day.

"May I have the body of the deceased?" I asked.

"Why?"

"Uh . . . for identification," I said.

"No, you may not. He escaped custody and is now AWOL."

"But you said he was dead."

"I didn't say that," he said.

"Yes, you did."

"Are you calling me a liar?"

"No, sir. I must have misunderstood. I will submit a correct roster tomorrow."

That day the entire company searched for hours trying to find a cockroach, any cockroach. Late that night, we found one, gently killed it, created a ditty bag for it, and scotch tapped its corpse to the front of the ditty bag. I then added Seaman Recruit Charley Cockroach to the company roster. Each morning thereafter, I made out a sick chit for Charley and placed him, his ditty bag, and sick chit next to the side of the formation.

About two weeks later, a guy named Squirrel went over the fence. An extensive amount of paperwork was required to report a missing man, and I listed him on the company roster as being AWOL. For three days, nothing happened. On the fourth day, I received official instructions, in triplicate, to drop Squirrel from the company roster. That was good—one less line to type on the roster. The man had disappeared, the paperwork was in order, and the paper monster was happy.

A week later, Charley went AWOL. I duly completed the paperwork in triplicate and changed Charley's status. True to form, four days later I received official instructions to drop Charley from the company roster. The paper monster was happy, and Charley was never heard from again.

Fed properly, the paper monster can be your friend.

The Airplane Non-Crash

"San Diego Center, this is American one-five-seven on final approach."
"Roger, one-five-seven; you are clear to land on runway two-seven-
zero. Report to ground control on frequency seven-eight-niner."
"Roger, San Diego; one-five-seven out."

Being in the navy requires a presence of mind. A sailor must always know where he is and be aware of his surroundings. I am sure they taught us that in boot camp, but I must have been filling out paperwork at the time.

The San Diego Naval Base was the cheapest land the navy could find. In practical terms, that meant no one else wanted it because it butted against the end of the San Diego Airport runway. The base also marked the boundary between the graceful rolling hills of Southern California and the coastal plane.

After boot camp I was assigned to a school on basic electronics. My barracks and the school bordered Rosecrans Street. I was moving up in the world because that was the beautiful part of the base. Although the central section of the base was swamp flat, this section rested on a slight rise up to a huge hill with a long, gentle slope leading to its peak. The lights from the civilian homes on the hillside sparkled like diamonds, and added depth and charm to the landscape.

I had taken some leave and checked in late on a Sunday evening. I was assigned an upper bunk on the second floor of a Spanish-style barracks. The sleeping area featured a vaulted roof room about ninety feet long and thirty feet wide. My guess is it held over two hundred men. The high, double hung windows that ran the length of the room provided the only air conditioning, and the resulting cross breeze precluded the use of curtains.

The room was lined on each side with white double bunks made from heavy bent pipes shaped like upside-down *U*'s welded together to make the head and foot of the bunk. Between the metal pipes were two galvanized steel bed frames topped by a two-inch thick mattress.

I had just enough time to stow my gear before lights out. I stretched out on my bunk face down and propped my shoulders against the pillow so I could gaze out the window across Rosecrans Street. The night was quiet, the street deserted, and the lights from the civilian homes twinkled brightly. The only sound was that of the cicadas chirping. I lay there absorbing the sweet ambiance of perfectly ordered barracks life as only a nineteen-year-old could.

In the distance, I picked up the sound of a distant jet. It grew closer and closer until the jet cleared the top of the hill. Suddenly the roar of its engines shattered the peaceful night. That didn't surprise me because I had spent my boot camp days being buzzed by the landings of commercial airliners. But I had never witnessed a landing like this one. I was blinded by two huge landing lights, one on each wing that shined white hot directly into my eyes. All I could see were the two landing lights, the tail, and wingtips. The pilot seemed to be fighting to regain his glide path because his rate of descent matched the slope of the hill. And I was at the bottom of that hill. If he didn't level out, the pilot and I would soon be eye to eye. The jet kept coming. Soon the screaming aircraft filled the entire sky. My bunk vibrated, and the plane's lights washed the barracks in a garish white light that formed long, sharp, black shadows. The plane wasn't leveling out.

That moment, lying in the harsh white light, was the darkest of my life. I knew I was about to die, the victim of a horrific airplane crash. Hundreds of others would die with me, but that was of little consequence then. The lights continued to bear down, the barracks' walls shook from the thundering engines. I had become mesmerized by the nature of my destruction, but finally, I snapped out of it. I wasn't going to die lying down; I had to escape, and escape would require some gymnastics. From a facedown position, I had to get up, reverse direction, and flee. I completed the gymnastic feat; then, remembering my comrades, I yelled, "Everyone hit the deck!"

I bolted, but I forgot to remember I was on the upper bunk. The result was a perfect one-point landing, a header. Meanwhile, the brightly burning bright lights were closer. (At this precise instant I was unaware that I was suffering from a temporal continuity gap. I was not in the barracks; I was in the emergency ward, and the light was from the doctor's penlight. He was checking my pupil reactivity. But all I knew was the lights were closer.)

I dove to the deck—again. In this, my second deck dive, I decked the doctor. Clutching the deck in a full body hug, I looked around to see a medical ward, not a soon-to-be-destroyed barracks. When things returned to normal, the doctor informed me I had a concussion; thankfully, the doctor didn't. Then came—you guessed it—the paperwork. In the navy, there's always more paperwork.

While the doctor filled out the paperwork, I reconsidered my actions and parked a tidbit of wisdom in the corner of my mind; once you hit the deck, you can't improve your position by hitting the deck again.

Staring at the clipboard, the doctor puckered his lips. "What should I put down as the cause of the accident?"

"I thought the airplane was going to crash."

"Well, it didn't, but it did cause your injury." The doctor's voice told me he was reasoning his way through a puzzle. After a second, his face lit up, and he scribbled on his clipboard.

"What'd you put down?"

"Injured in an airplane crash that never happened."

"That doesn't make any sense."

"No problem; this is the navy."

Praise the Lord, and Pass the Potato Chips

While living at the bottom of the navy's food chain and only taking home $80 a month, I needed to live frugally. That, I am convinced, was part of the navy strategy to keep young men out of trouble, and it worked to a degree. I once scrimped for six weeks to scratch enough together for a day out of town. Yes, I went to Tijuana, but in the name of decency, I'll skip that part. When you only have twenty bucks a week to spend life is tough, and barrack's life made it tougher.

Pudgy uniform munching silverfish infested the barracks forcing me to either buy bug spray for my locker or replace at least one of my white cotton uniforms weekly. I opted for bug spray as did everyone else. Aftershave was a lost cause; we all reeked of bug spray, which has about a ten-foot effective stench range. We saved money on toiletries and called ourselves the Raid Regiment, or the Raiders, which has a nice special-ops sound to it.

So, after deducting the cost of bug spray from my twenty dollar a week budget, finding ways to save money on liberty was essential.

Downtown San Diego, just up from fleet landing, was a wild and woolly place. It attracted young sailors like moths to a flame. There were a few blocks of raucous bars I couldn't afford, but what the heck, I was still underage. After the bars, the main drag became almost civilized. This civilized area is where I spent most of my liberty hours.

My favorite haunt was the movie theater on the square. It showed films twenty-four hours a day, and admission was only a buck or two. As a bonus, the ticket was good for the entire day, so you could come and go as you pleased. They served soda, chips, hot dogs, and hamburgers in the lobby, so if I decided to stay, I could enjoy a good weekend for a few bucks.

Mostly I remember fifties horror flicks about some huge surly insect or vegetable with a bad attitude toward homo sapiens. Radiation from nuclear tests not only made them mean, but caused a significant drop in the heroine's IQ. (Come on, what sane woman would go into a sandy desert wearing high heels and a tight skirt?) But what the heck, the theater was air conditioned.

Despite the low-class movies, the theater was a civil place; management only allowed sleeping in the balcony, which explains why it became crowded after ten in the evening. It wasn't much, but there weren't any petty officers around busting my ass every five minutes.

20

The theater solved my shelter and entertainment problems, but the bigger issue was food. Back then, buying the equivalent of a Big Mac would put my wallet into cardiac arrest. The Mission solved the food problem.

The Mission sat between the bars and the theater. I think the Mission's operators would have preferred being right in the middle of the bars, but that was probably the high rent district. The Mission would open its doors every hour, on the hour, from eleven in the morning to seven at night to welcome indigents and young, hungry sailors.

I always arrived ahead of time because once they let admitted forty souls, they closed their doors until the clocks chimed the next hour. The Mission interior consisted of a large, square room with a serving line on one end, a pulpit on the other, and about a dozen tables in between. A steel door stood in the wall behind the pulpit.

The Reverend kept the Mission rules simple: they locked you in for an hour, gave you all the sandwiches and soda you wanted, and at half past the hour, the Reverend delivered a sermon. Once the reverend appeared, they took all the food off the serving line, so stoking up before hand was mandatory.

Sounds heavenly doesn't, but I learned its dark sinister secrets on my first trip to the mission. I was standing in line waiting for the doors to open when the deepest baritone voice I've ever heard whispered in my ear, "Ya know, this is a KGB front."

Behind me stood the pre-production prototype of Arnold Schwarzenegger in marine uniform wearing aviator sunglasses. I knew he was a marine because in this, The Dark Ages, the military required servicemen to wear uniforms on liberty. "What?" I asked.

Deep Throat glanced over his shoulder and leaned in to me. "Yeah, KGB, they kidnap military personnel."

"Isn't this a religious mission?" I asked.

"That's what they want you to think; it's a perfect cover isn't it?"

For anyone raised in the Cold War era, the implications were clear. This was exactly the type of thing the godless evil Russian Empire would do. Visions of commie torture chambers with hypodermic needles and all kinds of bizarre medieval apparati used to extract military secrets from hapless servicemen flooded my mind. I took a solemn oath to defend my country from these guys. As a member of the US military in good standing, this new information conflicted me; I was hungry.

"Huh?" I asked.

"Quiet," Deep Throat said. "They just opened the doors." His voice was so deep it turned the whole world spooky and made my goose bumps shiver, but I was really hungry.

We worked our way through the slow moving food line and took a seat. Even though the reverend was probably a KGB Colonel I must give him credit for his oratorical skills. Compared to this guy, Winston Churchill sounded like Pee Wee Herman. His sermons started in a conversational tone and built uninterrupted for twenty minutes. By the end of the sermon, amid the scents of fire and brimstone that effused the room the Reverend shouted, pumped his arms, and banged his fists on the pulpit. At the climactic moment, he threw his right hand across his chest, thrust his left arm heavenward, and shouted, "Who wants to be saved?"

My heart thumped, and the urge to jump up and yell, "Amen," almost overwhelmed me, but his words clicked in my head. It was a silly question to ask a bunch of young, red-blooded American boys hell bent on sinning as much as possible before returning to base. Deep Throat was right. No true American would ask such a silly question. The knowing look Deep Throat gave me said, "See I told you so."

Congregation members swarmed the dining area and asked each diner if they wanted saving. I sat stiff in my chair, stared at my paper plate, and avoided eye contact. A congregation member bent over and asked me, "Do you want to be saved?"

The steel door loomed ominously. I'm a catholic, and we take the express line to confession when we need saving, so I yelled, "For the love of God and Country, I don't want to be saved."

In the following months, I witnessed many of my acquaintances declare for salvation, and once they said the fateful words, "I want to be saved!" Congregation members jerked the chair from under them, and hustled them through the steel door. After the steel door slammed shut behind them with an apocalyptic thud, I never saw any of them again.

Poor guys.

Maybe Deep Throat was right.

What the heck, the food was free if you kept your mouth shut.

Treasure Island

The navy likes its formations square and its lines straight. This thinking carries over into all navy endeavors, and the brass comes unglued when things aren't square or straight. That's why sailors spend so much time and effort figuring out how to beat the system by putting kinks into those straight lines. It drives the brass crazy and provides entertainment for the enlisted personnel. These things I learned on a square island in San Francisco Bay.

Yerba Buena Island sits in the middle of the bay. Being half-way between Oakland and San Francisco, it serves as the center support for the Oakland Bay Bridge and as a jumping-off point to visit Treasure Island.

Treasure Island was built for the 1930 World's Fair and was created by dredging the Sacramento River and dumping the silt on top of Frisco's garbage dump in the bay. But after the World's Fair, nobody wanted to buy a square, water-locked, reclaimed garbage dump that was difficult to access. Never fear, the US Navy was willing to help.

Treasure Island met all of the navy's base criteria: nobody wanted it; it was difficult to access; and the land was cheap. As a bonus, the navy got a free, reclaimed garbage dump. It was a deal made in heaven. On their newfound prize purchase the navy built the large training center that would be my next duty station.

The navy sent me there for training on RADAR systems as an electronics technician. The school was long and effective. After fifty-six weeks, I had the RADAR system schematics memorized. I also graduated with the highest grade point average on record. (Recall my warning, "The older I get the better I was.") I can't take any credit for my academic excellence; electronics just came easy to me, and I found a way to kink the navy's system.

Back then the navy had developed an effective motivational technique. Any student who failed a single exam would receive orders as a radioman on a patrol boat, riverine, or SWIFT boat stationed in the Mekong Delta of Vietnam—life expectancy, nine months. A SWIFT boat was small and ran contrary to my economic theories of survival, so even though the subject matter came easy to me, I studied hard.

I ripped through my first one-hundred-question multiple-choice exam in record time, so I was able to check my answers a couple of times. But with time still remaining in the exam period, I got bored, so I decided to count the number of A, B, C, and D answers on my answer sheet. I had twenty-five A and C answers, but five too many B's and five too few D's.

Hmmm. The navy likes everything to line up square, so I wondered if I checked my B answers if I might find five that I could reasonably change to D. When I finished, I had the same number of A's, B's, C's, and D's, and handed in my answer sheet; I aced the exam. Hmmmmmmm.

I repeated this procedure for the next twenty weeks and did well on each exam because my system raised my test scores by as much as twenty points. Little did I know the navy testing center had perfected the art of testing; that is, in a navy logic sort of way. They had a catalog of thousands of questions and statistical research that could predict the number of students who would be able to answer each question correctly.

In the world of the testing center, everything was perfect. They could construct exams that would produce a perfect bell curve simply by creating the right mix of questions. Apparently my system broke their bell curve. Someone in the testing center, probably a statistician, figured my grades were statistically impossible—unless I had the answer key.

The navy was convinced its system was so mathematically perfect it could even identify cheaters like me, but it wanted to make sure. The training center put together what is called a J-factor test. I never found out what the term meant, but the test was designed to be so tough it was statistically impossible for anyone to pass. But I did. I aced it. After all, it was an easy formula to follow; twenty-five A's, twenty- five B's, twenty-five C's, and twenty-five D's.

The morning following the J-factor test I was ordered to report to the training center and ushered into a large conference room that contained a single table about twenty-five feet long that was covered with a green felt tablecloth. There was enough gold braid in the room that I would have retired if I could have stolen all the uniforms.

They told me to sit at the end of the table in the only chair that didn't have a coffee cup or ashtray. About this time I figured something might be up, and it might have to do with my test scores. Speaking of economic odds of survival, I realized that if the navy thought I was cheating, I would be up the Mekong River without a SWIFT boat, a canoe, or a paddle, and my best chance at survival would be to volunteer as a target at target practice.

The guy with the most gold braid sat at the opposite end of the table facing me and opened the conversation with small talk. "Seaman Laswell, tell me where you are getting the answer keys to the exams. That's a direct order."

Nice to meet you, too, sir; and how's the misses?

"I haven't been getting answer keys from anyone, sir."

"You are in enough trouble now; don't make it worse by disobeying a direct order. I want the name of the individual or individuals who are giving you the answer keys," Gold Braid said.

"Sir, I would tell you where I am getting the answer keys if I were getting the answer keys, but I'm not. There's no way I can complete your order."

"No matter what happens, you are facing disciplinary charges, but if you don't tell me where you are getting the answer keys, I will have you court-martialed," Gold Braid said. All the other gold braids nodded.

This was not going well even though a court-martial and brig time would be better than the Mekong River without a paddle. Just then there was a knock on the door, and a senior petty officer entered: "I am Seaman Laswell's instructor, and I have known him for several months. May I speak?"

Gold Braid nodded, and what followed was the most eloquent thirty minute defense of Seaman Laswell's character, work ethic, aptitude, and other traits ever delivered. My mother would have believed all of it, and the instructor convinced Gold Braid of enough of it to get me off the hook.

On the walk back to the school building, I said, "Good thing you showed up; I thought I was a goner. Thanks a lot."

"Don't sweat it. They've got a bunch of overpaid civilian propeller heads back there who couldn't tell the difference between a sea bat and their ass."

"Well anyway, thanks a lot."

"Tell me though, honestly; you didn't cheat did you?"

"No way."

"That's a relief, but how do you do it?"

I told him my secret formula, and he burst out laughing.

"What's so funny?"

"Something I've known for years. Shore-based propeller heads are totally defenseless in a battle of wits with the ordinary sailor. Did you tell them how you did it?"

"No; they never asked."

"Good for you."

"You're not going to tell them, are you?"

"Hell, no. Let them figure it out. Someday those overpaid SOBs will earn their pay. Have you told anybody else about your system?"

"Are you kidding? What the heck would happen if the entire class used it? The brass would be in therapy for months."

"You've gotta point."

"Yeah, but I just realized something. If my grades start falling, they will figure I got scared off, and I was really cheating after all."

"Yup, you're in a corner. Better study your ass off."

Which I did for the next thirty-two weeks. That had a substantially negative impact on my poker playing time. But what the heck; I had better things to do with my money, anyway.

Fireworks on the Bay

The Treasure Island training center was home to the navy's only school on its most powerful RADAR system. Its power output was classified, but the word was it was in the megawatt range. How much is a megawatt? Enough for a psychedelic bay-wide light show.

The building where the navy held classes on this RADAR sat next to a high tower with a parabolic RADAR antenna on top. This antenna differed from other RADAR antennas because it rotated and could be aimed at any elevation from horizontal to almost perfectly vertical. Because of its power, the antenna was always pointing skyward.

The training building was an old WWII wooden building with a pitched roof. The pitched roof was a mystery to me; its green shingles were covered by a smattering of white blotches. At first I thought it was seagull droppings, but that was the only building with so much of the white stuff on it, so I figured it had to be something else, but what?

The sea legend about the RADAR was that it was so powerful, if someone threw a raw egg through the RADAR beam, the egg would be hard boiled instantly and then explode. I confirmed the sea legend one evening at the mess hall. I had sat down at the picnic-style tables with my metal tray full of food. The guy across from me was busy shoveling mashed potatoes into his mouth, so I asked him the standard conversation starter, "Been here long?"

"'Bout a year. How 'bout you?"

"Three months. You getting orders any time soon?"

"Naw; I'll be here another six months, then I'm probably headed for a greyhound."

"Been on destroyers before?"

"Yup, two tours."

"So what're you doing here?" I asked.

"Instructor. I'd lived on the beach, but my old lady ditched me."

"Tough luck. What do you teach?"

"The SPX-985."

That was the big, powerful radar.

"I hear it can make an egg explode if you throw one through the beam."

"True. True."

"How do you know?"

My dinner companion stopped, cocked his head, and gave me a crooked smile. "Cause I did it. It's a bitch trying to throw an egg from the ground

27

through an invisible moving beam, especially when you've had a few beers. Took two dozen eggs before I got it right. Yeah, the egg just goes POW! Makes a neat sound when it explodes, though."

With the legend confirmed, I put the matter out of mind and never questioned the white stuff on the building roof again.

A few weeks later, I pulled the midwatch to guard the RADAR training building from midnight to four in the morning. I always felt that such duty was chicken shit; why should I have to guard a building that had done fine without me for over twenty years? I concluded the navy was afraid a Russian commando team would swoop in and steal it. To prevent this, they posted a single unarmed guard on the building, which was absurd, so it made perfect sense in a navy-logic way.

Denied the comfort of a warm bed and half asleep, I trudged through the cool night toward my watch station knowing full well I would spend the next four hours walking circles around the radar building. The wind from the bay made me scrunch my head and neck down into my peacoat to stay warm. Standing a watch like that was stupid, served no purpose whatsoever, and was the brasses' way of harassing the troops. Don't get me wrong; had there been a valid reason to guard the building I would have gladly stood my watch with motivated vigilance. To maintain my morale and sanity, I tried to dream up a valid reason why I had to walk in circles for four hours in the middle of the cold night. I failed.

Facing the miserable prospect of walking in circles for four hours, I continued my trudge to the RADAR building. Dead ahead was the Oakland Bay Bridge, glowing like a Christmas tree lit by hundreds of sodium vapor lamps. Then I noticed the lights on the bridge nearest Oakland flickered and grew brighter. Lights exploded in golden fireballs, sending showers of bright white sparks in every direction. Whatever was happening, it was marching across the bridge like a string of firecrackers headed toward San Francisco.

I looked up at the RADAR antenna. It was pointed horizontal to the ground, not skyward.

I ran into the school building and found the transmitter room containing the instructor and former dinner mate with several students. "You're in radiate with a horizontal beam. You're blowing up the bay bridge!" I yelled over the sound of the equipment.

"Shut down!" the instructor yelled before dashing out the door. I followed, and what to my wondering eyes did appear—fits and spits and sparks from well-toasted, and now extinct, mercury vapor lights on the Bay Bridge. The RADAR beam was creeping across the skyline of downtown

San Francisco. As it crawled across the city, the fluorescent lights in the downtown skyscrapers filled windows with bright, eerie light.

That was a once-in-a-lifetime event, and I was at ground zero—the epicenter—of a polished brass, four gold star f**k up with oak leaf cluster. It was awesome.

The instructor simply said, "Pretty, ain't it." And he wore that cockeyed grin again.

"Sure is. You're gonna need a bucket of Vaseline before this is over."

"Wouldn't be the first time, but what the heck; it's not bad unless they put sand in it. Good thing you saw it, though," the instructor conceded. "Why were you out here this late?"

"Guard duty," I said, puffing out my chest. "It's my job to stop people from throwing eggs on the roof."

Haight-Ashbury

It was the sixties, the Age of Aquarius when peace would rule the planets and love would steer the stars. Hippies, pot, LSD, and "Make love not war" were in their ascendancy. It was a time when you could do your own thing, and "Peace" was the universal greeting and farewell.

The Temple Mount of the hippie movement was the area of San Francisco named for its main cross streets, Haight and Ashbury. That's what the map said, but on the street, those headed to Haight-Asbury would say, "Just going to the street called love, man. Peace."

The navy, never known for its open-mindedness, declared hippies and Haight-Ashbury off limits to all navy personnel. The navy didn't understand putting such an iconic location off limits made it a must-see for every young sailor. I swear I never would've visited Haight-Ashbury if the navy had ordered me to go.

If Haight-Ashbury was the Temple Mount, then Ashbury Street running from Oak to Fredrick was the sanctuary. The northern end of Ashbury comes to a T on Oak Street that forms the southern boundary to the calm, verdant Golden Gate Park Panhandle. Haight, the east-west street, reaches its western terminus at Golden Gate Park only five blocks west.

On Ashbury, you could find anything you ever wanted be it animal (hippie), mineral (LSD), or vegetable (pot). Pot, which sold at five bucks a lid, was delivered in plastic sandwich bags. LSD, which sold by the tab for ten bucks, was delivered as a white dot of powder on a small piece of paper.

Ashbury street was as mixed up as the hippies who claimed it as their home. My overarching memory is that it was a drab and dirty place punctuated by colored lights and even more colorful and energetic people. To stroll the sidewalks of Ashbury, one had to accept the shoulder bumps, pedestrian collisions, backups, and the unique aroma of the street, all of which peaked at the intersection of Haight and Ashbury.

Visitors were welcomed into a light, joyful street fair atmosphere. On a warm, humid summer's night the street took on a gentle back-alley aroma, and no one was more than an arm's length away from smoke or clothing with a heavy, distinctive, earthy, and pungent odor of sweet skunk or burnt sage. Chatting people stood in clusters, forming pinball-like obstacles for window shoppers, dog walkers, looky-loos, and those just out for a walk.

Everyone was cool or, should I say, at least semi-stoned. Odd behavior was normal and never garnered special attention. After all, everyone had the right to do his or her own thing. Dancing to the eerie, screeching psychedelic music from one of the many shops was normal fare, as was the occasional individual dancing to the music blaring in his head from a never-never land named LSD. Haight-Ashbury was the type of place wannabes cruised from the safety of their cars.

The residents of Ashbury gave me the impression they hadn't showered in weeks. Their hair was long and unkempt, and the scragglier the better. The men were particularly interesting because you could only see their eyes framed by a head of long hair and the obligatory scruffy beard. At times the sidewalk looked like a procession of eyes peering out of Calder-like hair haystack mobiles.

Typical male dress was jeans, a dark shirt, and an army fatigue coat or a jacket of similar cut. The braless women wore long, flowing dresses, and I can't recall any of them being colorful prints; my memory only sees dark colors. Shoes were optional, and sandals were the standard. These denizens of Ashbury, distant cousins of Homo sapiens, were a bedraggled and scruffy bunch. I spent many an hour just people watching; surprise, astonishment, or curiosity was never more than a minute away.

One evening a short-haired haystack approached me. The haystack pulled his hand from his army fatigue jacket, pointed his finger gun at me and said, "Bang."

I pulled my finger gun, took careful aim, and said, "Boom. Boom."

The blast from my finger gun nearly lifted the haystack from the pavement. The impact spun him a full 360 degrees, and he fell face first onto the concrete like a felled sequoia. That was an interesting response to my act of self-defense. Nevertheless, I continued my walk toward Golden Gate Park. An hour later when I returned, people were nonchalantly walking around the haystack's body. Physically, he was there, but his mind had left on a trip to where he could do his thing; he'd be back before dawn.

The buildings lining Ashbury were devoid of the vibrant colors of San Francisco, and they hid their beauty and classic architecture beneath drab paint and dirty siding. Lining the sidewalks were shops of every description: head shops, cafes, poster shops, and tourist shops where you could buy the latest in hippie clothing. The typical shop was a sparsely stocked room with counters and displays around the back walls. The cluttered store windows were as diverse as the activities on the street. Always colorful and bright, the store windows ranged from mundane to bright psychedelic. Flashing lights, especially strobes, were common.

The strobe lights seemed to attract those flying on LSD like moths. One night I passed a hair haystack kneeling on the sidewalk, nose pressed against the window, mesmerized by a strobe light not six inches from his eyes. Motionless, he kept his hands splayed against the window on either side of his head. He remained as still as a statue for hours before passing out. No one thought anything of it; it was a normal night on the street called love.

Commerce was always evident on the sidewalk. Every few feet people would be hawking their wares: pot, LSD, a *Berkeley Barb* underground newspaper, or their bodies for the price of a lid or a tab. Those selling their bodies sickened me because many of the young women seemed to be of high school age, and all they wanted was to get high. To this seedy side of Ashbury, add dog excrement and litter to the sidewalks to complete a picture quite different than what the flower children promised.

Into this drab but energetic place I ventured clean and beardless with my military haircut, conservative middle-class dress, and my spit-shined dress uniform shoes. To say I stood out in the crowd would be an understatement, and this is when my fascination with Haight-Ashbury began. It wasn't the place; it was the people and their ideals.

This was perhaps an idyllic period before the My Lai and Kent State massacres that brought hate to the street called love as taunts of "murderer" and "baby killer" were thrown at military personnel. Despite my outward appearance, which screamed MILITARY, the hippies accepted me without question. If there was magic in Haight-Ashbury, that was it. The culture was, without exception, devoid of bias or stereotypes. Everyone accepted every race, opinion, and viewpoint. I had my thing, they had their thing, and everyone was cool with that. No one judged anyone.

During my many visits, I found new friends and, for a time, enjoyed the company of Mary Jane, a five-foot-two beauty with luxurious blonde hair cascading off her shoulders past her waist. She favored dresses of dark red and burgundy. This Ashbury sprite loved to slow dance on the street to sitar music, sensuously swaying her body between liquid, expressive arms. She was the only one I saw who could draw a crowd.

I saw her negotiating the price of a lid with a street vendor. It seemed she was a buck short, so I intervened and gave her the dollar she needed. She followed me like a puppy for a block before I stopped to talk with her. She found me fascinating in a "What's a nice guy like you doing in a place like this?" way. I found her intelligent, witty mind captivating. Later, she admitted her name wasn't Mary Jane, but she wouldn't tell me her real name. Well, that was her thing, and I was cool with that, just as she was cool with my haircut and spit-shined shoes.

For one shining moment perhaps peace did rule the planets, and perhaps love did steer the stars in a confusing place named Haight-Ashbury.
Peace.

English Lightning

Only two times in my life has a beer made an impression on my psyche that lasted forty years. The first beer was English Lightning (I have changed the name to protect the guilty). The second beer, San Miguel, would come a few years later when I was deployed on a destroyer. In retrospect, I find this an interesting turn of events because I had the opportunity to savor the finest beers Germany had to offer, and I can't remember the name of a single one. But I will never forget English Lightning and San Miguel.

I don't know if they still make English Lightning, and society would be better off if they didn't, but I was introduced to this Bay Area beer on a Friday night at a drive-in movie. An Oakland drive-in was running an all-night marathon of the *Man with No Name* trilogy starring Clint Eastwood. One of the guys in my outfit had a car, so four of us piled in and headed across the Bay Bridge toward Oakland. We figured we would need something stronger than soda from the snack bar, so we stopped at a local store to get some beer. Being frugal, we asked the owner which was the best beer for the buck. His reply was unequivocal, "English Lightning."

It seemed that English Lightning only came in six-packs of sixteen ounce cans, so each of us picked one up. We had some misgivings wondering if one six-pack would be enough to hold each of us through an all-night marathon. The owner assured us one six-pack would be enough; after all, they were sixteen ounce cans.

My first sip of English Lightning expanded my definition of beer beyond any previous limit of credulity. This stuff was *fortified*. Think high-octane racing fuel that left a lingering, bitter barley aftertaste. Being indestructible young men, no one commented on the beer. Instead, we munched our way through our buckets of popcorn while watching *The Good, the Bad and the Ugly* and enjoying the Ennio Morricone soundtrack and our English Lightning beer. But I never saw the end of the movie.

The next thing I remember was the attendant banging his hand on the roof of the car. It was painfully daylight, the marathon was over, and the attendant demanded we leave. I felt like hammered shit, and every gravel pothole to the exit sent an English Lightning bolt through my skull. On the way back to base, we took inventory. Only one of us had finished two cans. That was Dave, and we couldn't wake him up. Two of us had finished one can and barely started another. Thankfully, the driver hadn't lasted long enough to finish his first can.

34

The Marine guard at the gate confiscated our thirteen unopened cans of English Lightning, which was fine with us. The Marines could have it, and it served them right for being Marines. We carried Dave back into the barracks and deposited him in his bunk, making sure all of his appendages were aboard the mattress. I took a bottle of aspirin and ran aground face-first into my pillow. My head was still achy at breakfast Sunday morning.

That was my first and last experience with English Lightning, and I have often wondered if it should be banned by treaty as a weapon of mass destruction. Just imagine what would happen if we shipped a truckload of that stuff to the enemy the night before an attack. No, we couldn't do that; after sampling the beer, the judge at the Hague would undoubtedly rule it a war crime.

I have a hangover just writing about it.

Shrubbery Inn

My economic situation improved somewhat after I left San Diego. I had become a third-class petty officer, and I could afford to buy food in reasonable restaurants, but housing on the beach was still beyond my reach.

During a weekend excursion to Haight-Ashbury, housing was necessary because the trip back to Treasure Island was three bus rides long and took too much time. On my first few weekend trips, I chose to stay at the "shrubbery inn" in Golden Gate Park.

Golden Gate Park, a great place for a lazy weekend stroll, was a world away from Haight-Ashbury. It was calm and quiet. There I could enjoy the shade of stately trees, vast expanses of cool grass, and a reasonable night's sleep hidden in the shrubbery.

The shrubbery inn was free, and it had its quirks. First, I always had to bring a jacket to sleep on, even in the summer. Next was the etiquette. When selecting a particular shrub to crawl under, I had to make sure it was not occupied, and if it was, I had to be careful not to wake the occupant. The big problem was the police patrol cars—at least until you learned the system.

Police cars patrolled the park on a regular basis at night to keep it safe and roust out any undesirables sleeping in the shrubbery. The police cars would cruise as slowly as turtles, and their driver's-side spotlights would dart about in the darkness to probe the darker moon shadows and the shrubbery. It didn't matter how well you concealed yourself; those guys were professionals. My first roust went like this:

"Hey, you, come out of there."

"Who, me?"

"Yes, you. Get out here where I can see you."

"What's the matter, officer?"

"You can't sleep in the park; it's against the law."

"Sorry, I didn't know that."

"Where you from?"

"Ohio."

"What are you doing here in California?"

"Stationed at Treasure Island."

"You in the navy?"

"Yes, sir."

"Got any ID?"

"Yes, sir . . . Here."

"Okay, I'm not going to run you in or get you in trouble with the navy, but you have to find someplace else to sleep. You can't sleep here."

"Okay, I'll find someplace else to sleep."

"Good. Now move on."

I moved on slowly wondering what to do. I decided to find a new shrub, but the park was crowded and all the good spots were taken. I began to wonder why the cop had left them alone and singled me out. At the last shrub I checked, I found out when I accidentally kicked the occupant.

"Hey, what are you doing?"

"Sorry, just trying to find a place to sleep. The cops ran me out of the bushes I was in."

"Just go back there and go to sleep."

"Can't they just run me off again?"

"Dumb ass. They checked you out, didn't they?"

"Yeah."

"Once they know you're okay, they'll leave you alone."

I returned to my original bush and hunkered down. I didn't go to sleep because I didn't trust the advice I'd been given. I figured if I got rousted again, I could claim I had returned to find something I had lost. But sure enough, when the cruiser came by the next time, the police shot their spotlight right at me and kept going. I slept well the rest of the night.

The next night I found a different set of bushes and settled in for the night. I was rousted thirty minutes later. After the cop left, I crawled back into my bush and had another good night's sleep.

On my next weekend trip, I stayed at the same bush both nights and only got rousted once, on Friday night. Apparently, one roust bought you a weekend pass—as long as you didn't change bushes.

Zookie

My weekend sleeping arrangements improved a few weeks later. I was at the all-night cafe just one door south of the Haight-Ashbury intersection on the west side of Ashbury. The cafe was crowded that night, but I did find an open booth of aquamarine and white Formica that dated back to the fifties. I was enjoying my usual five-course meal of French fries, hamburger, cheese, bread, and ketchup when a hair haystack approached.

"Mind if I sit there?" the haystack asked pointing to the empty bench across from me.

The appropriate answer was, "Whatever, man," but I looked at his eyes. His voice seemed normal, but if he was coming off a bad LSD trip, being near him could be hazardous.

"Whatever, man," I said. His eyes seemed okay. My evaluation of him wouldn't have changed my answer, but it could have hastened my departure.

The hair haystack put the red plastic open weave basket containing his five-course dinner on the table and took a seat. "I'm Zookie."

"Hi."

"What's your name?"

"Larry," I said.

"Too bad. Got a middle name?"

"Keith."

"Sorry. What do you want to be called?"

"Whatever."

"Okay, I'll call you 'Whats.'"

"Whatever."

"You by yourself?"

"Don't know. Mary Jane could drop in any time."

Zookie looked at me for a second, probably wondering if I was waiting for some weed or a girl. Zookie cleared his throat and said, "You waiting on her?"

"Not really; she comes and goes as she pleases. If she sees me in here, she'll probably pop in for a visit."

"You military?"

"How'd you guess?"

"The glasses gave you away. I thought this place was dangerous for you guys."

Zookie was not referring to any threat coming from the neighborhood. He meant the navy.

"I just have to be careful. I have a security clearance, and the word is if they catch me with drugs, they'll lock me up until all the information I have access to is declassified."

"That's harsh, man. With a bummer like that hangin' over your head, what 'cha doin' here?"

"I'll only have one chance to experience this, and I find the people fascinating."

"You mean stoned?"

"Well, that too, but that's different than being fascinating. For example, you got a degree?"

Zookie took a conspiratorial look around the room before replying, "Master's in English lit."

"Got a job?"

"Reporter for the *Chronicle*."

"See what I mean. You don't look like a master's degree or literature type, and certainly not a newspaper man."

"True, true."

"Who's your favorite author?"

Over a second round of sodas, Zookie regaled me for the next hour about Chaucer, Shakespeare, and a gaggle of other classic authors. His grasp of literature was firm and piercing, his elocution perfect, and his arguments compelling and articulate. He was a man I wanted to know, and certainly not one to be judged by his appearance. He was typical Haight-Ashbury.

When we finished our second sodas, he asked, "You headed back to base?"

"Naw, I'll stay until tomorrow."

"Where you staying?"

"Shrubbery inn."

"Bummer. You want a nice warm place to stay, 'cause I can fix you up."

"Sure, but I don't have much money."

"No problem, man. You can't buy your way into this place, but you can share your way in."

"What do you mean?"

"Come on; we'll get you a six-pack, and then I'll show you."

Zookie led me to a shop where I purchased a six-pack of beer before heading to a second floor walk-up. "When you get in," Zookie said, "just set the beer down anywhere."

When the door opened, the scent of burning hemp hit me like a wrecking ball; I inhaled deeply. The flat had a living room large enough for a blue oversized couch, two beige overstuffed chairs, a TV, and a few tables. Every table held an ashtray, but the largest ashtray sat in the middle of a threadbare brown-and-gold rug spread across the hardwood floor. With sheets for drapes and hand-me-downs for furniture, I feared I had just stepped into a flop house. But it was far from it; the place was spotless, the kitchen neat, and the bedroom off-limits. Zookie reached into his pocket and dropped two lids on the floor. I sat my six-pack down next to his offering.

No one seemed to notice us or what we had placed on the floor, but one by one the other six occupants reached out and shared our offering.

Zookie took me aside and said, "That's it, man. Bring something to share, and you're good for the night. Let me introduce you to your new friends so you can mix in and enjoy."

I was instantly part of the group, and no one asked about my spit-shined shoes. Later, one hair haystack offered me a toke off his joint, but I deferred: "Don't need it; all I have to do is take a few breaths." Everyone got a chuckle out of that.

With my jacket as a pillow, I had a long peaceful sleep that night. What the heck—I was young, the floor wasn't that hard, and the price of lodging was within my reach. As a bonus, I got stoned without taking a single toke, and as far as I knew, secondhand smoke wasn't illegal—even in the navy.

To My Readers

Thank you for reading *A Ship-load of Sea Stories & 1 Fairy Tale Volume 1*. I hope you enjoyed it and will recommend it to your friends. I am a self-published author, and reviews are a powerful way to spread the word about books you enjoy. I would be grateful for your support if you would take a few minute to leave a review on Amazon or other book sites.

There will be many more volumes of *A Ship-load of Sea Stories & 1 Fairy Tale*. If you want me to let you know when the next volume is released, go to my website at http://larrylaswell.com and sign-up for my email list.

Don't be afraid to email me through my website or comment on my blog. I enjoy meeting my readers and sharing ideas. You can also stay in touch with me on Facebook, Twitter, and LinkedIn or go to my website, LarryLaswell.com. I have four novels in the pipeline, and the easiest way to learn about my new novels is to subscribe to my mailing list or blog RSS feed.

Now that you've finished my first installment of A Ship-load of Sea Stories & 1 Fairy Tale, you might enjoy my first novel in *The Marathon Watch*. Just turn the page to read the first chapter.

Thank you again, and good reading.

Larry Laswell

Contact Me!

Website:	http://LarryLaswell.com
Facebook:	http://bit.ly/larryfacebook
Twitter:	@larrylaswell
LinkedIn:	http://bit.ly/LarryLinkedIn
Amazon:	http://bit.ly/LarryOnAmazon
Email Sign-up:	http://bit.ly/LarrysEmailPage

Larry always gives his fans a special deal on new books, so sign-up here for email notifications.

Breakdown

August 1971, The Aegean Sea off the coast of Greece
Operation Marathon: Day 399

Ross hated August north of the equator. The hot, humid August days made engine room conditions almost unbearable. The USS *Farnley*'s engine room ran hotter than most others, and today, August served up its hottest day yet.

Seated on a battered wooden bench, Master Chief Machinist Mate Ross kept an eye on his throttlemen. Stucky and Burns both jerked their throttle valve open another eighth turn. That was the third time in the last past five minutes, but their speed held steady. Things weren't adding up.

Ross scanned the twenty-odd gauges mounted on the white enameled board above the throttlemen's heads. Steam pressure held at six hundred pounds, temperature at six-eighty, and vacuum at twenty-nine inches. The readings seemed okay. *I must be getting paranoid,* he thought.

Out of habit, Ross checked the gauge board again. This time he didn't see the gauges; instead, he took in the entire board. A year ago, the white enameled steel board had glistened; now it was covered in grease and grime. The board disgraced him. He told himself he didn't care. It was impossible to maintain his self-esteem aboard this bucket. It wasn't worth the effort.

Ross bent forward to rest his elbows on his knees and think. He hated the *Farnley* and wished he could forget the last year of his life. Except for dreaming about the day he would leave this ship, his present assignment held no hope and no pleasant memories.

Why the navy decided to shaft the *Farnley*, her crew, and him was a mystery. It wasn't fair; that wasn't part of the deal. He was tired and wanted to get off the *Farnley* and out of the navy. He just needed to survive eleven more months without screwing up.

Do your time, retire, and escape.

Ross' mind wandered, but the feeling that something was wrong pulled him back. He twirled his screwdriver in his fingers to give him something to do. Dozens of problems worth worrying about could cause an increase in steam demand.

Why should I care? This isn't my engine room, and it isn't my ship.

Elmo, a cockroach and engine room mascot, scurried across the deck plates toward the bench, providing Ross a welcome diversion. On any other ship, Elmo would be a problem but not on the *Farnley*. Ross told himself he didn't care and shook his head to convince himself.

Hundreds of roaches infested the engine room and thousands infested the ship, but everyone knew Elmo. The crew envied his gift for not caring and for not being bothered by anything. Like all cockroaches, Elmo was the quintessential survivor, so the crew accepted him as a fellow shipmate and honored him. After painting a single red chevron on his back, they gave him the honorary rank of petty officer third class.

In a sharp movement, Stucky spun his throttle open an additional half turn.

"Stucky, what's your speed?" Ross yelled over the noise.

Stucky checked his shaft tachometer and turned his head to see Ross. "One hundred ten revolutions. Making turns for ten knots."

"You been holding steady?"

"Absolutely, Chief."

"Then why do you keep opening the throttle?"

Stucky shrugged. "Don't know. Didn't think it was worth worrying about."

Ross hated the words *not worth*. Most everything on the *Farnley* was not worth doing or worth worrying about or worth the effort. Every time he said those words to himself, a piece of him died, but it wasn't worth the fight; he couldn't win.

Burns jerked his throttle open a quarter turn. Something's wrong, he thought. You always tell your men, "Always stay alert down here. Your life and your shipmates' lives depend on it. The machinery can eat you alive. The high-voltage wiring can fry you, and six-hundred-pound steam'll cook you dead in seconds."

Pay attention.

Ross scanned the gauge board again. The condenser vacuum was falling. The problem centered on the condenser. Ross thought he could make out a high-pitched sound barely audible over the noise, but he couldn't be sure. He strained to pick the sound out of the cacophony. It eluded him. Perhaps it was something he felt, or he might have been imagining it. Nothing was ordinary on the *Farnley*. The engine room was full of sick equipment making unnatural noises.

The sound Ross heard came back a bit louder. The tormented scream was familiar, and his ears picked the sound out of the chaotic racket. What was it? Screaming in agony, a bearing sang its high-pitched song of death. The hair on the back of his neck stood up, and the shock wave of adrenaline blasted through his body. The main condensate pump was about to seize.

With only one of four pumps operational, the situation was critical. If the pump failed, a wall of water would back into the steam turbines. When solid water hit the high-speed turbine blades, the result would be explosive. The resulting hail of hot metal shards would tear a human body to bits. For anyone aft of the gauge board, death would be horrific and instantaneous.

Ross bolted from his position and slid down the ladder to the lower level. His feet hit the lower catwalk deck plates with a metallic bang. Heads turned.

He yelled, "Clear the lower level! Everyone forward! Now!"

Dropped tools rattled into the bilge as firemen clattered across the web of catwalks. Ross kept moving. He flung himself over the railing and dropped the last four feet into the bilge. His feet splashed in the half inch of black, oily water. He was right; the high-pitched sound he heard was coming from the condensate pump.

Despite his forty-seven years, Ross vaulted over the catwalk guardrail and ran up the ladder to the main level. On the main level, he pushed through the excited firemen, reached for the bridge intercom, and yelled, "Bridge, Main Control! Request all-stop. We've got a problem down here with the condensate pump."

The reply was immediate. "Main Control, this is the captain. Negative on the all-stop. If you have a problem down there, fix it."

Shit, why is the captain always on the bridge? Ross thought for a second and pressed the send button again.

"Captain, this is Ross. If we lose the pump, we lose power and probably damage the pump. We need time. I told you this might happen with only one pump."

"Chief, if you have a problem, fix it. You're not stopping my ship in the middle of the ocean so you can baby one of your pumps. We're going to continue making turns on both screws. Those are my orders. Do you understand?"

"I can't stop the inevitable. Christ, Captain! You could kill somebody down here."

"Chief, it's not inevitable for someone who knows what he's doing. I'm tired of your insubordination and won't take any more. You have your orders. Make them so."

A year earlier, Ross would have bristled at those words. He wanted to now, but his pride failed him. It was no use arguing with an ass like Captain Javert.

What's the use? It's his ship, not mine. Eleven more months. Survive. Follow orders.

Ross hit the send button again. "Aye, aye, Captain."

To the six firemen huddled behind the gauge board, Ross said, "All of ya, out of here. Get me a cup of coffee or something, but get back quick when the lights go out."

Ross turned his attention to the gauges as the six men scrambled up the ladder like terrified plebes. Stucky, still at his throttle, wiped his sweaty hands on his tattered dungarees. "What now, Chief?" he asked.

"Stay on your toes."

The expression on Stucky's freckled face told Ross he hadn't answered the question. Without looking, Ross knew the eyes of the four remaining men were asking the same question. "You're safe forward of the gauge board," he yelled so everyone would hear.

Ross thought about warning Fireman Canterbury and his boiler room crew. With only fourteen months aboard the *Farnley*, Canterbury was the senior man on the boiler team. Ross cursed to himself. By normal standards, it takes four years' experience to run a boiler crew. Damn this ship! Ross knew what was going to happen. No danger there.

Ross stepped onto the wooden bench and stretched to reach the wheel on the main steam stop valve. His hands slipped on the warm, oily metal of the thirty-inch valve wheel. He wiped his hands on his trousers and tried again. This time, his purchase held. With a hand on each side of the valve wheel, Ross stood spread-eagled. He listened and waited.

The scream of the bearing became clearly audible. Ross braced himself to close the valve to shut off the flow of steam. The bone-chilling screech from the pump peaked. Ross tugged at the valve wheel. It gave a few inches, then jammed.

The pump's scream rose to a crescendo and abruptly ended as the pump seized. The turbines' whine turned into a growing deep, ominous growl. Within seconds, the turbines would explode. "All-stop! Close the throttles," Ross screamed as loud as he could.

The growl of the turbines held steady for a second, then died away as the panic-stricken throttlemen closed their valves.

Ross pursed his lips as the dial on the steam pressure gauge inched toward the danger zone. The boiler room crew wasn't paying attention.

§

In the boiler room, the boilers continued to produce steam with nowhere to go. The boiler room crew, standing in glazed-eyed boredom, didn't notice. Within seconds, the boiler pressure rose to almost seven hundred pounds and forced the safety valves open.

The explosive venting of steam through the stacks blocked out all other sensations. The sound possessed the boiler room. Canterbury's organs shook, his stomach quaked, and his lungs tingled from the vibration. Scarcely aware of the warm, moist burst of urine on his leg, Canterbury yanked the boiler's emergency kill switch. He was the fourth of six men up the escape ladder.

§

Deprived of steam, the electric generators spun to a stop, and the ship went dark. In Main Control, Ross waited for the battle lanterns to click on. Deprived of electricity, the *Farnley*'s motors, blowers, and other equipment went silent. Only the distant lapping sound of the ocean and an occasional echo from a drop of water falling into the bilge could be heard. A wave of angry despair washed the energy from his body.

This wasn't the deal. It wasn't the way his navy worked. He wanted to be able to do his job, to teach and mentor his crew. He wanted his pride and sense of accomplishment back. The heartbreaking silence shamed Ross.

Stucky turned toward Ross. "What happened, Chief?"

With a tired, fluid movement, Ross retrieved his screwdriver and turned toward the freckle-faced sailor. "Son, we've just done got *Farnley*ed. Again."

§

Minutes earlier, perched in his captain's chair, Commander Alan Javert carefully released the intercom's send button with his left toe, then froze in position as he listened to Ross' reply of "Aye, aye, Captain." He worried that the bridge crew would notice his awkward movement. He hated his Ichabod Crane body because it made it difficult to look and move like other ships' captains. Careful to make his movements deliberate but graceful, he withdrew his foot from the intercom and settled back into his chair to study the horizon.

Despite his effort, the movement still felt awkward. It was impossible to make his long, skinny legs move with the sure grace of an athlete. He told himself his body wasn't his fault and focused his thoughts on what to do next. He didn't know what to do. Mentally he panicked. What could he do? What should he do? Why was the world against him?

Javert couldn't tolerate challenges to his authority. He was the captain. He had to be decisive; that's what captains were. He couldn't fall behind schedule and let the world know he couldn't get the job done. Fearful the bridge crew would see through him, he kept his outward appearance calm as if he'd accepted Chief Ross' "Aye, aye, Captain" as a *fait accompli.*

The knot in Javert's stomach hardened into a painful, tight ball of muscle, and dizziness swept over him. Fearful he would fall from the chair, he clenched the arms with both hands. He riveted his eyes on the horizon and hoped its stability would give him equilibrium. He fidgeted and tried to compose himself. Composure was another captainly trait he tried to imitate.

46

The *Farnley*'s problems weren't his fault. He was a good captain with the experience and qualifications for command. His real problem was the incompetent group of disloyal officers and men the navy had given him. Other captains wouldn't put up with the derelicts he'd been given. He'd done the right thing by putting Ross in his place, but that didn't fix the pump. He had to do something. Other captains would. If he didn't do something quickly, the crew would know he didn't know what to do.

Anxiously, Javert turned to look across the gray, shadowy bridge to find Biron, the conning officer. All he could see was shadows. Half panic-stricken, he started to get out of his chair until he spotted the brown smudge of a khaki uniform in the distance. Standing on the far bridge wing, Biron leaned on the rail and calmly watched the sea. Reassured of Biron's location, Javert cleared his throat and settled back into his chair. What have I done wrong? he wondered.

When Javert had taken command of the *Farnley*, he'd forgotten about the cliquish nature of a destroyer crew like the *Farnley*'s or the *Renshaw*'s, where he'd been the gunnery officer during the Korean War. At OCS, they told him that the unique culture aboard a ship was almost tribal. He remembered how the crew revered the captain, loved him, respected him, feared him, and would die for him. At the time, he'd assumed crews always treated their captains that way because captains demanded it. Now he understood he had had it backwards; the crew demanded it of the captain. The captain had to come up to the crew's standards.

Javert tried to be likable, and failing at that, he tried to earn their respect by being commanding. That wasn't working either. Javert suspected the men had lost respect for him. He could see it in their looks, and he heard it in Ross' voice. They no longer followed his orders willingly or paid attention to his wishes. He'd done everything he thought other captains would do. Still, it wasn't enough.

The abrupt roar of escaping steam rent the quiet evening air. At first, Javert thought a CO_2 fire extinguisher had discharged, but the sound was far too loud.

The status board keeper went rigid. "Sir, aft lookout reports lifting safeties."

Biron, already back on the bridge, shouted, "Very well!" as he headed for the intercom. Passing the helmsman, he yelled, "All-stop. Rudder amidships."

The roaring sound of escaping steam stopped as suddenly as it had begun. As Biron reached for the intercom, relays clicked, and in unison, red indicator lights dimmed, then blinked out. The ship went silent, lifeless, dead in the water.

Javert, self-conscious about his awkward body, resisted the urge to stand. Carefully controlling his voice, he turned to Biron and said, "Find out what happened and get it fixed. Get the emergency diesel started so we have power. I won't allow us to fall behind schedule."

Without power, the intercom was useless. Biron removed the sound-powered telephone handset from its cradle and turned his back to Javert. "Bridge, Main Control. What's your status?"

Javert squinted at the darkness as the aft bridge door opened and a man entered. Javert recognized the boxerlike silhouette as that of Lieutenant Commander Meyers, the *Farnley*'s executive officer. Many people mistook Meyers for a marine due to his thick neck and muscular upper body. Even in silhouette, he was hard to miss. Meyers hurried toward Javert and Biron. "What happened?" Meyers asked.

Biron lifted his head slightly. "Dropped the load. Diesel generator is coming online. Condensate pump, I think."

Biron lowered his head, directing his attention to the phone. "Bridge, aye." He looked around Meyers to locate Sweeney, the boatswain's mate of the watch. "Sweeney, tell the lookouts to be sharp. We don't have radar, and our running lights are out."

Placing the phone in its cradle, Biron leaned back against the wood sill so he could speak to both men. "Dropped the load. The emergency generator . . ." he paused as the distant, hesitant popping rumble of the diesel steadied out, ". . . is online. We should be back on steam in five. Ross says it'll take fifteen to assess the damage. We seized a bearing in the number two condensate pump."

A few indicator lights beamed back to life. The muted bell of the engine order telegraph clinked, and the lee helmsman called out in a subdued, almost apologetic, voice, "Sir, engine room answers all-stop."

Biron didn't speak but nodded his acknowledgment to the lee helmsman. Meyers shook his head in disgust.

Javert dropped from his chair and stepped directly in front of Meyers, forcing Biron out of the way. With his shoulders hunched and neck thrust forward, Javert squinted down at Meyers. "XO, this is unsat. It's your job to see that these things don't happen. Brief me when you find out how long repairs will take. Once we get the problem fixed, I want to know how you're going to keep us on schedule. I'll be in my cabin. Do you understand?"

Meyers' voice was businesslike. "Yes sir. And you'll have the breakdown message in a few minutes."

"No! XO, we've been over this before about breakdown reports. I told you, they're only required if we can't keep our schedule. We don't know that yet, so no report."

"Captain—"

Javert ignored Meyers' plea and stormed off the bridge, yelling, "I'll be in my cabin, XO. You have your orders. Make them so."

About Larry

Larry Laswell served in the US Navy for eight years. In navy parlance, he was a mustang, someone who rose from the enlisted ranks to receive an officer's commission. While enlisted, he was assigned to the USS *John Marshall* SSBN-611 (Gold Crew). After earning his commission, he served as main engines officer aboard the USS *Intrepid* CV-11. His last assignment was as a submarine warfare officer aboard the USS *William M. Wood* DD-715 while she was home ported in Elefsis, Greece.

In addition to writing, Larry, a retired CEO, fills his spare time with woodworking and furniture design. He continues to work on *The Marathon Watch* series, an upcoming science fiction series titled *The Ethosians*, and an anthology of over eighty humorous sea stories titled *A Ship-load of Sea Stories & 1 Fairy Tale*.

Website:	http://LarryLaswell.com
Facebook:	http://bit.ly/larryfacebook
Twitter:	@larrylaswell
LinkedIn:	http://bit.ly/LarryLinkedIn
Amazon:	http://bit.ly/LarryOnAmazon
Email Sign-up:	http://bit.ly/LarrysEmailPage

www.ingramcontent.com/pod-product-compliance
Lightning Source LLC
Chambersburg PA
CBHW071219130626

46555CB00004B/1763